Eileen Chang

LUST, CAUTION

Eileen Chang (Zhang Ailing) was born in Shanghai, China, in 1920. She studied literature at the University of Hong Kong but in 1941, during the Japanese occupation, she returned to Shanghai, where she published *Romances* (1944) and *Written on Water* (1945), which established her reputation as a literary star. She moved to Hong Kong in 1952 and in 1955 to the United States, where she continued to write. She died in Los Angeles in 1995.

ALSO BY EILEEN CHANG

Love in a Fallen City

The Rouge of the North

Written on Water

LUST, CAUTION

LUST, CAUTION

The Story

Eileen Chang

Translated and with a Foreword by Julia Lovell

AFTERWORD BY ANG LEE
WITH A SPECIAL ESSAY BY
JAMES SCHAMUS

ANCHOR BOOKS
A Division of Random House, Inc.
New York

AN ANCHOR BOOKS ORIGINAL, AUGUST 2007

Cataloging-in-Publication Data
is available at the Library of Congress.

ISBN: 978-0-307-38744-8

Book design by Rebecca Aidlin

www.anchorbooks.com

Printed in the United States of America
10 9 8 7 6 5 4 3 2 1

FOREWORD

Julia Lovell

"To be famous," the twenty-four-year-old Eileen Chang wrote, with disarmingly frank impatience in 1944, "I must hurry. If it comes too late, it will not bring me so much happiness. . . . Hurry, hurry, or it will be too late, too late!" She did not have long to wait. By 1945, less than two years after her fiction debut in a Shanghai magazine, a frenzy of creativity (one novel, six novellas, and eight short stories) and commercial success had established Chang as the star chronicler of 1940s Shanghai: of its brashly modern, Westernized landscapes populated by men and women still clinging ambivalently to much older, Chinese habits of thought. "The people of Shanghai," she considered, "have been distilled out of Chinese tradition by the pressures of modern life; they are a deformed mix of old and new. Though the

result may not be healthy, there is a curious wisdom to it."

Chang's own album of childhood memories was a casebook in conflict between the forces of tradition and modernity, from which she would draw extensively in her writing. The grandson of the nineteenth-century statesman Li Hung-chang—a high-ranking servant of China's last dynasty, the Ch'ing—her father was almost a cliché of decadent, late-imperial aristocracy: an opium-smoking, concubine-keeping, violently unpredictable patriarch who, when Eileen was eighteen, beat and imprisoned his daughter for six months after an alleged slight to her stepmother. Her mother, meanwhile, was very much the kind of Westernized "New Woman" that waves of cultural reform, since the start of the twentieth century, had been steadily bringing into existence: educated and independent enough to leave her husband and two children behind for several years while she traveled Europe—skiing in the Swiss Alps on bound feet. After Chang's parents (unsurprisingly) divorced when she was ten, the young Eileen grew up steeped in the strange, contradictory glamour of pre-Communist Shanghai: between the airy brightness of her mother's modern apartment and the languid, opium smoke–filled rooms of her father's house.

Yet while Chang's fiction was eagerly devoured by the Shanghai readers for whom she wrote—the first edition of her 1944 collection of short stories sold out within four days—it drew carping criticism from literary contemporaries. For Eileen Chang wrote some way outside the intellectual mainstream of the middle decades of twentieth-century China. Although an early-twenty-first-century Western reader might not immediately notice it from much of her 1940s fiction—the body of work for which she is principally celebrated—she grew up and wrote in a period of intense political upheaval. In 1911, nine years before she was born, the Ch'ing dynasty was toppled by a revolutionary republican government. Within five years, this fledgling democracy collapsed into warlordism, and the 1920s through '40s were marked by increasingly violent struggles to control and reform China, culminating in the bloody Sino-Japanese War and civil conflict between the right-wing Nationalists and the Chinese Communist Party. Many prominent Chinese writers of these decades—Lu Hsün, Mao Tun, Ting Ling, and others—responded to this political uncertainty by turning radically left-ward, hoping to rouse the country out of its state of crisis by bending their creative talents to ideo-logically prescribed ends.

Despite experiencing firsthand the national cataclysms of the 1940s—the Japanese assault on Hong Kong and occupation of north and east China (including her native Shanghai)—Eileen Chang, by contrast, remained largely apolitical through these years. Although her disengaged stance was in part dictated by Japanese censorship in Shanghai, it was also infused with an innate skepticism of the often overblown revolutionary rhetoric that many of her fellow writers had adopted. In the fiction of her prolific twenties, war is no more than an incidental backdrop, helping to create exceptional situations and circumstances in which bittersweet affairs of the heart are played out. The bombardment of Hong Kong, in her novella *Love in a Fallen City,* serves only to push a cynical courting couple to finally commit to each other. In the short story "Sealed Off," two Shang-hai strangers—a discontented married man and a lonely single woman—are drawn into conversa-tion in the dreamlike lull that results while the

Japanese police perform a random search on the tram in which they are traveling.

Defying critics who scorned her preoccupation with "love and marriage . . . leftovers from the old dynasty and petty bourgeois" and her failure to write in rousing messages of "youth, passion, fantasy, hope," Chang instead argued for the subtler aesthetics of the commonplace. Writing of "trivial things between men and women," of the thoughts and feelings of ordinary, imperfect people struggling through the day-to-day dislocations caused by war and modernization, she contended, offered a more acutely realistic portrait of the era's desolate transience than did patriotic demagoguery. "Though my characters are not heroes," she observed, "they are the ones who bear the burden of our age. . . . Although they are weak—these average people who lack the force of heroes—they sum up this age of ours better than any hero. . . . I don't like stark conflicts between good and evil . . . we should perhaps move beyond the notion that literary works should have 'main themes.'" Eileen Chang was one of the relatively few writers of her period who adhered to the belief, throughout her career, that the business of the fiction writer lay in sketching out plausibly complex, conflicted individuals—their confusions, frustrations, disappointments, and selfishness—rather than in attempting uplifting political advocacy. "This thing called reality," she meditated in a deadpan account of the bombing of Hong Kong, "is unsystematic, like seven or eight phonographs playing at the same time, each its own tune, forming a chaotic whole. . . . Neatly formulated visions of creation, whether political or philosophical, are bound to irritate."

Chang's lack of interest in politics and inevitable antipathy toward the strident aesthetics of socialist realism efficiently guaranteed her exclusion from the Maoist literary canon and impelled her to leave China itself. In 1952, three years after the Communist takeover, as the political pressures on her grew, she decided to abandon her beloved Shanghai, first for Hong Kong and then for the United States, where she lived and continued to write until her death in 1995. In the post-Mao literary thaw, even as Mainland publishers and readers delightedly rediscovered Chang's sophisticated tales of pre-1949 Shanghai and Hong Kong, critics were still unable to rid themselves of long-standing prejudice against her, belittling her work for its neglect of the "big issues" of twentieth-century China: Nation, Revolution, Progress, and so on.

Begun in the early 1950s, finally published in 1979, "Lust, Caution" in many ways reads like a long-considered riposte to the needling criticisms by the Mainland Chinese literary establishment that Chang endured throughout her career, to those who dismissed her as a banal boudoir realist. For while the story carries all the signature touches that marked Chang as a major talent in her early twenties—its attentiveness to the sights and sounds of 1940s Shanghai (clothes, interiors, streetscapes); its cattily omniscient narrator; its deluded, ruthless cast of characters—it adds an intriguingly new element to this familiar mix. In it, Chang created for the first time a heroine directly swept up in the radical, patriotic politics of the 1940s, charting her exploitation in the name of nationalism and her impulsive abandonment of the cause for an illusory love. "Lust, Caution" is one of Chang's most explicit, unsettling articulations of her views on the relationship between tidy political abstraction and irrational emotional reality—on the ultimate ascendancy of the latter over the former. Chia-chih's final, self-destructive change of heart, and Mr. Yee's repayment of her gesture, give the story its arresting originality, transforming a polished espionage narrative into a disturbing meditation on psychological fragility, self-deception, and amoral sexual possession.

For until its last few pages, "Lust, Caution" functions happily enough as a tautly plotted, intensely atmospheric spy story. A handful of lines into its opening, Chang has intimated, with all the hard-boiled economy of the thriller writer, the harsh menace of the Yees' world: the glare of the lamp, the shadows around the mahjong table, the flash of diamond rings, the clacking of the tiles. Brief exchanges establish characters and relationships: the grasping Yee Tai-tai, the carping Ma Tai-tai, the obsequious black capes, the discreetly sinister Mr. Yee. Chia-chih's entanglement with her host is exposed with the slightest motion of a chin, her coconspirators introduced through a brief, cryptic telephone conversation, the plot's two-year backstory outlined in a few paragraphs. At times, the reader struggles to keep up with the speed of Chang's exposition, as characters and entanglements are mentioned then left swiftly behind: the disappointing K'uang Yu-min; the seedy Liang Jun-sheng; the bland Lai Hsiu-chin, Chia-chih's only other female coconspirator; the shadowy Chungking operative Wu.

The suspense reels us steadily along, through the wait in the café, the stage-managed visit to the jewelry store and the ascent to the office, and into the story's startling finale—the section to which Chang is said to have returned most often over almost three decades of rewriting. Chang draws us artfully into her heroine's delusion, enveloping Chia-chih's progression toward her error of judgment in the sweet, stupefying air of the dingy jeweler's office. Afterward we follow Chia-chih on her sleepwalk out of the store, sharing her surreal confidence that she will be able to escape quietly for a few days to her relative's house, until we wake at the shrill whistle of the blockade and the abrupt braking of the pedicab. Mr. Yee's return to the mahjong table brusquely exposes the true scale of Chia-chih's miscalculation: his ruthless, remorseless response, his warped sense of triumph. "Now that he had enjoyed the love of a beautiful woman, he could die happy—without regret. He could feel her shadow forever near him, comforting him.

Even though she had hated him at the end, she had at least felt something. And now he possessed her utterly, primitively—as a hunter does his quarry, a tiger his kill. Alive, her body belonged to him; dead, she was his ghost."

This final free indirect meditation echoes with Chang's ghostly, sardonic laugher—mocking not only her weak, self-deceived heroine, but also her own gullible attachment to an emotionally unprincipled political animal. For Chang's obsessive reworking of Chia-chih's romantic misjudgment was, at least in part, autobiographically motivated. Like Chia-chih, Eileen Chang was a student in Hong Kong when the city fell to the Japanese in 1942, and she, too, subsequently made her way to occupied Shanghai. Also like Chia-chih, shortly after her return to Shanghai, she entered into a liaison with a member of the Wang Ching-wei government—with a philandering literatus by the name of Hu Lan-cheng, who served as Wang's Chief of Judiciary. In 1945, a year after the two of them entered into a common-law marriage, the Japanese surrender and collapse of the collaborationist regime forced Hu to go into hiding in the nearby city of Hangzhou. Two years later, having supported him financially through his exile, Chang painfully broke off relations with him on discovering his adultery.

Far beyond its specific autobiographical resonances, though, the story's skeptical disavowal of all transcendent values—patriotism, love, trust—more broadly expresses Chang's fascinatingly ambivalent view of human psychology: of the deluded generosity and egotism indigenous to affairs of the heart. In "Lust, Caution," the loud, public questions—war, revolution, national survival—that Chang had for decades been accused of sidelining are freely given center stage, then exposed as transient, alienating, and finally subordinate to the quiet, private themes of emotional loyalty, vanity, and betrayal.

A NOTE ON NAMES

There are two main systems for romanizing Chinese in English: Wade-Giles, developed at the end of the nineteenth century and widely used up until the 1970s, and pinyin, introduced by the People's Republic of China in 1979. Because of its subject matter and use of language, "Lust, Caution" is powerfully evocative of pre-Communist China, so the older system has been used throughout this translation, with the exception of the surname Yee (for which the Wade-Giles version, "I," might have distractingly confused readers) and a few of the place-names (Chungking, Tientsin, Nanking), for which the English transliterations most commonly used in the 1940s have been given, again in the interest of creating a period mood.

And here, finally, is a list of characters, in

order of appearance in the text, to assist the reader in pronouncing and remembering the Chinese names. Pronunciations are as written, unless otherwise specified in the parentheses following each name.

Wang Chia-chih (*Chia* pronounced as "jam" without the "m"; *chih* as the "ger" in "larger"): A student actress turned assassin's plant; Mr. Yee's seductress.

Mai Tai-tai: Wang Chia-chih's cover-name in the conspiracy—the Tai-tai (wife) of a fictional Hong Kong businessman, Mr. Mai.

Wang Ching-wei (*Ching* as "jing" in "jingle"; *wei* as "way"): A real historical figure, Wang formed a Chinese collaborationist government in Japanese-occupied Nanking between 1940 and 1944.

Yee Tai-tai (Ee Tie-Tie): The wife of Mr. Yee, the Wang Ching-wei government minister targeted by the student plotters.

Ma Tai-tai: A member of Yee Tai-tai's regular mahjong circle.

Liạo Tai-tai (Lee-ow Tie-Tie): Another member of Yee Tai-tai's mahjong circle.

Mr. Lee: An acquaintance of the Yees in Shanghai.

Mr. Yee (Ee): The head of Wang Ching-wei's intelligence service and the target of the assassination plot; Wang Chia-chih's lover.

Chou Fo-hai (Joe Foe-hi): A real historical figure, Wang Ching-wei's second-in-command in the wartime collaborationist government.

K'uang Yu-min (Kwang You-mean): The leader of the student conspirators.

Liang Jun-sheng (Leeyang Rune-shung): Another student conspirator; briefly Wang Chia-chih's lover, forced on her by the circumstances of the plot.

Huang Lei (Hwang Lay): The wealthiest student conspirator.

Ou-yang Ling-wen (*Ou* as in "oh"; *wen* as "wan" in "rowan"): Another student conspirator.

Lai Hsiu-chin (Lie Show-jin): The only other female student involved in the plot.

Wu (Woo): A member of the anti-Japanese underground resistance in Shanghai, with connections to the Nationalist government in Chungking.

—*Julia Lovell*

LUST, CAUTION

Though it was still daylight, the hot lamp was shining full-beam over the mahjong table. Diamond rings flashed under its glare as their wearers clacked and reshuffled their tiles. The tablecloth, tied down over the table legs, stretched out into a sleek plain of blinding white. The harsh artificial light silhouetted to full advantage the generous curve of Chia-chih's bosom, and laid bare the elegant lines of her hexagonal face, its beauty somehow accentuated by the imperfectly narrow forehead, by the careless, framing wisps of hair. Her makeup was understated, except for the glossily rouged arcs of her lips. Her hair she had pinned nonchalantly back from her face, then allowed to hang down to her shoulders. Her sleeveless cheongsam of electric blue moiré satin reached to the knees, its shallow, rounded collar standing only half an inch tall, in the Western style. A brooch fixed to the collar matched her diamond-studded sapphire button earrings.

The two ladies—*tai-tais*—immediately to her left and right were both wearing black wool capes, each held fast at the neck by a heavy double gold chain that snaked out from beneath the cloak's turned-down collar. Isolated from the rest of the world by Japanese occupation, Shanghai had elaborated a few native fashions. Thanks to the extravagantly inflated price of gold in the occupied territories, gold chains as thick as these were now fabulously expensive. But somehow, functionally worn in place of a collar button, they managed to avoid the taint of vulgar ostentation, thereby offering their owners the perfect pretext for parading their wealth on excursions about the city. For these excellent reasons, the cape and gold chain had become the favored uniform of the wives of officials serving in Wang Ching-wei's puppet government. Or perhaps they were following the lead of Chungking, the Chinese Nationalist regime's wartime capital, where black cloaks were very much in vogue among the elegant ladies of the political glitterati.

Yee Tai-tai was *chez elle,* so she had dispensed with her own cape; but even without it, her figure still seemed to bell outward from her neck, with all the weight the years had put on her. She'd met Chia-chih two years earlier in Hong Kong, after she and her husband had left Chungking—and the Nationalist government—together with Wang Ching-wei. Not long before the couple took refuge on the island, one of Wang Ching-wei's lieutenants, Cheng Chung-ming, had been assassinated in Hanoi, and so Wang's followers in Hong Kong were keeping their heads down. Yee Tai-tai, nonetheless, was determined to go shopping. During the war, goods were scarce in both the unconquered interior and the occupied territories of the Mainland; Yee Tai-tai had no intention of wasting the golden purchasing opportunity offered by a stopover in the commercial paradise of Hong Kong. Someone in her circle introduced her to Chia-chih—the beautiful young wife of Mr. Mai, a local businessman—who chaperoned her on her shopping trips. If you wanted to navigate Hong Kong's emporiums, you had to have a local along: you were expected to haggle over prices even in the biggest department stores, and if you couldn't speak Cantonese, all the traders would overcharge you wickedly. Mr. Mai was in import-export and, like all business-people, delighted in making political friends. So of course the couple were incessantly hospitable to Yee Tai-tai, who was in turn extremely grateful. After the bombing of Pearl Harbor and the fall of Hong Kong, Mr. Mai went out of business. To make some extra money for the family, Mai Tai-tai decided to do a little smuggling herself, and traveled to Shanghai with a few luxury goods—watches, Western medicines, perfumes, stockings—to sell. Yee Tai-tai very naturally invited her to stay with them.

"We went to Shu-yü, that Szechuanese restaurant, yesterday," Yee Tai-tai was telling the first black cape. "Mai Tai-tai hadn't been."

"Oh, really?"

"We haven't seen you here for a few days, Ma Tai-tai."

"I've been busy—a family matter," Ma Tai-tai mumbled amid the twittering of the mahjong tiles.

Yee Tai-tai's lips thinned into a smile. "She went into hiding because it was her turn to buy dinner."

Chia-chih suspected that Ma Tai-tai was jealous. Ever since Chia-chih had arrived, she had been the center of attention.

"Liao Tai-tai took us all out last night. She's been on such a winning streak the last couple of days," Yee Tai-tai went on to Ma Tai-tai. "At the restaurant, I bumped into that young Mr. Lee and his wife and invited them to join us. When he said they were waiting for guests of their own, I told him they should all join us. After all, it isn't often that Liao Tai-tai gives dinner parties. Then it turned out Mr. Lee had invited so many guests we couldn't fit them all around our table. Even with extra chairs we couldn't all squeeze in, so Liao Tai-tai had to sit behind me like a singsong girl at a banquet. 'What a beauty I've picked for myself tonight,' I joked. 'I'm too old a piece of tofu for you to swallow,' she replied. 'Old tofu tastes the spiciest,' I told her! Oh, how we laughed. She laughed so much her pockmarks turned red."

More laughter around the mahjong table.

While Yee Tai-tai was still updating Ma Tai-tai on the goings-on of the past couple of days, Mr. Yee came in, dressed in a gray suit, and nodded at his three female guests.

"You started early today."

He stood behind his wife, watching the game. The wall behind him was swathed in heavy, yellowish-brown wool curtains printed with a brick-red phoenix-tail fern design, each blade almost six feet long. Chou Fo-hai, Wang Ching-wei's second in command, had a pair; and so, therefore, did they. False french windows, and enormous drapes to cover them, were all the rage just then. Because of the war, fabrics were in short supply; floor-length curtains such as those hanging behind Mr. Yee—using up an entire bolt of cloth, with extra wastage from pattern matching—were a conspicuous extravagance. Standing against the huge ferns of his backdrop, Yee looked even shorter than usual. His face was pale, finely drawn, and crowned by a receding hairline that faded away into petal-shaped peaks above his temples. His nose was distinguished by its narrowed, almost ratlike tip.

"Is that ring of yours three carats, Ma Tai-tai?" Yee Tai-tai asked. "The day before yesterday, P'in Fen brought a five-carat diamond to show me, but it didn't sparkle like yours."

"I've heard P'in Fen's things are better than the stuff in the shops."

"It is convenient to have things brought to your home, I suppose. And you can hold on to them for a few days, while you decide. And sometimes she has things you can't get elsewhere. Last time, she showed me a yellow kerosene diamond, but *he* wouldn't buy it." She glanced icily at Mr. Yee before going on: "How much do you imagine something like that would cost now? A perfect kerosene diamond: a dozen ounces of gold per carat? Two? Three? P'in Fen says no one's selling kerosene or pink diamonds at the moment, for any price. Everyone's hoarding them, waiting for the price to get even more insane."

"Didn't you feel how heavy it was?" Mr. Yee laughed. "Ten carats. You wouldn't have been able to play mahjong with that rock on your finger."

The edges of the table glittered like a diamond exhibition, Chia-chih thought, every pair of hands glinting ostentatiously—except hers. She should have left her jadeite ring back in its box, she realized; to spare herself all those sneering glances.

"Stop making fun of me!" Yee Tai-tai sulked as she moved out one of her counters. The black cape opposite Ma Tai-tai clatteringly opened out her winning hand, and a sudden commotion of laughter and lament broke the thread of conversation.

As the gamblers busily set to calculating their wins and losses, Mr. Yee motioned slightly at Chia-chih with his chin toward the door.

She immediately glanced at the two black capes on either side of her. Fortunately, neither seemed to have noticed. She paid out the chips she had lost, took a sip from her teacup, then suddenly exclaimed: "That memory of mine! I have a business appointment at three o'clock, I'd forgotten all about it. Mr. Yee, will you take my place until I get back?"

"I won't allow it!" Yee Tai-tai protested. "You can't just run away like that without warning us in advance."

"And just when I thought my luck was changing," muttered the winning black cape.

"I suppose we could ask Liao Tai-tai to come over. Go and telephone her," Yee Tai-tai went on to Chia-chih. "At least stay until she gets here."

"I really need to go now." Chia-chih looked at her watch. "I'm going to be late—I arranged to have coffee with a broker. Mr. Yee can take my place."

"I'm busy this afternoon," Mr. Yee excused himself. "Tomorrow I'll play all night."

"That Wang Chia-chih!" Yee Tai-tai liked referring to Chia-chih by her full maiden name, as if they had known each other since they were girls. "I'll make you pay for this—you're going to treat us all to dinner tonight!"

"You can't let your guest buy you dinner," Ma Tai-tai objected.

"I'm siding with Yee Tai-tai," the other black cape put in.

They needed to tread carefully around their hostess on the subject of her young houseguest. Although Yee Tai-tai was easily old enough to be Chia-chih's mother, there had never been any talk of formalizing their relationship, of adopting her as a goddaughter. Yee Tai-tai was a little unpredictable, at the age she was now. Although she had a dowager's fondness for keeping young, pretty women clustered around her—like a galaxy of stars reflecting glory onto the moon around which they circulated—she was not yet too old for flashes of feminine jealousy.

"All right, all right," Chia-chih said. "I'll take you all out to dinner tonight. But you won't be in the party, Mr. Yee, if you don't take my place now."

"Do, Mr. Yee! Mahjong's no fun with only three. Play just for a little, while Ma Tai-tai telephones for a replacement."

"I really do have a prior engagement." Whenever Mr. Yee spoke of official business, his voice sank to an almost inaudibly discreet mutter. "Someone else will come along soon."

"We all know how busy Mr. Yee is," Ma Tai-tai said.

Was she insinuating something, Chia-chih wondered, or were nerves getting the better of her? Observing him smile and banter, Chia-chih even began to read a flattering undertone into Ma Tai-tai's remark, as if she knew that he wanted other people to coax the details of his conquest out of him. Perhaps success, she speculated, can turn the heads of even the professionally secretive.

It was getting far too dangerous. If the job wasn't done today, if the thing were to drag on any longer, Yee Tai-tai would surely find them out.

He walked off while she was still exhaustingly negotiating her exit with his wife. After finally extricating herself, she returned briefly to her room. As she finished hurriedly tidying her hair and makeup—there was too little time to change her clothes—the maidservant arrived to tell her the car was waiting for her at the door. Getting in, she gave the chauffeur instructions to drive her to a café; once arrived, she sent him back home.

As it was only midafternoon, the café was almost deserted. Its large interior was lit by wall lamps with pleated apricot silk shades, its floor populated by small round tables covered in cloths of fine white linen jacquard—an old-fashioned, middlebrow kind of establishment. She made a call from the public telephone on the counter. After four rings, she hung up and redialed, muttering "wrong number" to herself, for fear the cashier might think her behavior strange.

That was the code. The second time, someone answered.

"Hello?"

Thank goodness—it was K'uang Yu-min. Even now, she was terrified she might have to speak to Liang Jun-sheng, though he was usually very careful to let others get to the phone first.

"It's me," she replied in Cantonese. "Everyone well?"

"All fine. How about yourself?"

"I'll be going shopping this afternoon, but I'm not sure when."

"No problem. We'll wait for you. Where are you now?"

"Hsia-fei Road."

"Fine."

A pause.

"Nothing else then?" Her hands felt cold, but she was somehow warmed by the sound of a familiar voice.

"No, nothing."

"I might go there right now."

"We'll be there, don't worry. See you later."

She hung up and exited to hail a pedicab.

If they didn't finish it off today, she couldn't stay on at the Yees'—not with all those great bejeweled cats watching her every move. Maybe she should have found an excuse to move out as soon as she had hooked him. He could have found her a place somewhere: the last couple of times they'd met in apartments, different ones each time, left vacant by British or Americans departed to war camps. But that probably would have made everything even more complicated—how would she have known what time he was coming? He might have suddenly descended upon her at any moment. Or if they had fixed a time in advance, urgent business might have forced him to cancel at the last minute. Calling him would also have been difficult, as his wife kept a close eye on him; she probably had spies stationed in all his various offices. A hint of suspicion and the whole thing would be undone: Shanghai crawled with potential informers, all of them eager to ingratiate themselves with the mighty Yee Tai-tai. And if Chia-chih had not pursued him so energetically, he might have cast her aside. Apartments were a popular parting gift to discarded mistresses of Wang Ching-wei's ministers. He had too many temptations jostling before him; far too many for any one moment. And if one of them weren't kept constantly in view, it would slip to the back of his mind and out of sight. No: he had to be nailed—even if she had to keep his nose buried between her breasts to do it.

"They weren't this big two years ago," he had murmured to her, in between kisses.

His head against her chest, he hadn't seen her blush.

Even now, it stung her to recall those knowing smirks—from all of them, K'uang Yu-min included. Only Liang Jun-sheng had pretended not to notice how much bigger her breasts now looked. Some episodes from her past she needed to keep banished from her mind.

It was some distance to the foreign concessions. When the pedicab reached the corner of Ching-an Temple and Seymour roads, she told him to stop by a small café. She looked around her, on the off chance that his car had already arrived. She could see only a vehicle with a bulky, charcoal-burning tank parked a little way up the street.

Most of the café's business must have been in takeout; there were hardly any places to sit down inside. Toward the back of its dingy interior was a refrigerated cabinet filled with various Western-style cakes. A glaringly bright lamp in the passageway behind exposed the rough, uneven surface of the brown paint covering the lower half of the walls. A white military-style uniform hung to one side of a small fridge; above, nearer the ceiling, hung a row of long, lined gowns—like a rail in a secondhand clothing store—worn by the establishment's Chinese servants and waiters.

He had told her that the place had been opened by a Chinese who had started out working in Tientsin's oldest, most famous Western eatery, the Kiessling. He must have chosen this place, she thought, because he would be unlikely to run into any high-society acquaintances here. It was also situated on a main road, so if he did bump into someone, it would not look as suspicious as if he were seen somewhere off the beaten track; it was central enough that one could plausibly be on one's way to somewhere entirely aboveboard.

She waited, the cup of coffee in front of her steadily losing heat. The last time, in the apartment, he had kept her waiting almost a whole hour. If the Chinese are the most unpunctual of people, she meditated, their politicians are surely virtuosos in the art of the late arrival. If she had to wait much longer, the store would be closed before they got there.

It had been his idea in the first place, after their first assignation. "Let's buy you a ring to celebrate today—you choose it. I'd go with you myself, if I had the time." Their second meeting was an even more rushed affair, and he had not mentioned it again. If he failed to remember today, she would have to think of artful ways of reminding him. With any other man, she would have made herself look undignified, grasping. But a cynical old fox like him would not delude himself that a pretty young woman would attach herself to a squat fifty-year-old merely for the beauty of his soul; a failure to express her material interest in the affair would seem suspicious. Ladies, in any case, are always partial to jewelry. She had, supposedly, traveled to Shanghai to trade in feminine luxuries. That she should try to generate a little extra profit along the way was entirely to be expected. As he was in the espionage business himself, he probably suspected conspiracies even where they didn't exist, where no cause for doubt had been given. Her priority was to win his trust, to appear credible. So far they had met in locations of his choosing; today she had to persuade him to follow her lead.

Last time he had sent the car on time to fetch her. The long wait she had had to endure today must mean he was coming himself. That was a relief: if they were due to tryst in an apartment, it would be hard to coax him out again once they were ensconced. Unless he had planned for them to stay out late together, to go out somewhere for dinner first—but he hadn't taken her to dinner on either of the previous two occasions. He would be wanting to take his time with her, while she would be getting jittery that the shop would close; but she wouldn't be able to hurry him along, like a prostitute with a customer.

She took out her powder compact and dabbed at her face. There was no guarantee he'd be coming to meet her himself. Now that the novelty had worn off, he was probably starting to lose interest. If she didn't pull it off today, she might not get another chance.

She glanced at her watch again. She felt a kind of chilling premonition of failure, like a long snag in a silk stocking, silently creeping up her body. On a seat a little over the way from hers, a man dressed in a Chinese robe—also on his own, reading a newspaper—was studying her. He'd been there when she had arrived, so he couldn't have been following her. Perhaps he was trying to guess what line of business she was in; whether her jewelry was real or fake. She didn't have the look of a dancing girl, but if she was an actress, he couldn't put a name to the face.

She had, in a past life, been an actress; and here she was, still playing a part, but in a drama too secret to make her famous.

While at college in Canton she'd starred in a string of rousingly patriotic history plays. Before the city fell to the Japanese, her university had relocated to Hong Kong, where the drama troupe had given one last public performance. Over-excited, unable to wind down after the curtain had fallen, she had gone out for a bite to eat with the rest of the cast. But even after almost everyone else had dispersed, she still hadn't wanted to go home. Instead, she and two female classmates had ridden through the city on the deserted upper deck of a tram as it swayed and trundled down the middle of the Hong Kong streets, the neon advertisements glowing in the darkness outside the windows.

Hong Kong University had lent a few of its classrooms to the Cantonese students, but lectures were always jam-packed, uncomfortably reminding them of their refugee status. The disappointing apathy of average Hong Kong people toward China's state of national emergency filled the classmates with a strong, indignant sense of exile, even though they had traveled little more than a hundred miles over the border to reach Hong Kong. Soon enough, a few like-minded elements among them formed a small radical group. When Wang Ching-wei, soon to begin negotiating with the Japanese over forming a collaborationist government back on the Mainland, arrived on the island with his retinue of supporters—many of them also from near Canton—the students discovered that one of his aides came from the same town as K'uang Yu-min. Exploiting this coincidence, K'uang sought him out and easily struck up a friendship, in the process extracting from him various items of useful information about members of Wang's group. After he had reported his findings to his coconspirators, they resolved after much discussion to set a honey trap for one Mr. Yee: to seduce him, with the help of one of their female classmates, toward an assassin's bullet. First she would befriend the wife, then move in on the husband. But if she presented herself as a student—always the most militant members of the population—Yee Tai-tai would be instantly on her guard. Instead, the group decided to make her the young wife of a local businessman; that sounded unthreatening enough, particularly in Hong Kong, where men of commerce were almost always apolitical. Enter the female star of the college drama troupe.

Of the various members of the group, Huang Lei was the wealthiest—from family money—and he briskly raised the funds to build a front for the conspiracy: renting a house, hiring a car, borrowing costumes. And since he was the only one of them able to drive, he took the part of chauffeur. Ou-yang Ling-wen was cast as the businessman husband, Mr. Mai; K'uang Yu-min as a cousin of the family, chaperoning the lovely Mai Tai-tai on her first meeting with Yee Tai-tai. After taking K'uang and the obligingly talkative aide back home, the car then drove the two ladies on to the Central District, to go about their shopping alone.

She had seen Mr. Yee a few times, but only in passing. When they finally sat down in the same room together—the first time the Yees invited her to play mahjong with them—she could tell right away he was interested, despite his obvious attempts to be circumspect. Since the age of twelve or thirteen, she had been no stranger to the admiring male gaze. She knew the game. He was terrified of indiscretion, but at the same time finding his tediously quiet life in Hong Kong stifling. He didn't even dare drink, for fear the Wangs might summon him for duty at any moment. He and another member of the Wang clique had rented an old house together, inside which they remained cloistered, diverting themselves only with the occasional game of mahjong.

During the game, the conversation turned to the fabric Yee Tai-tai had bought to make suits for her husband. Chia-chih recommended a tailor who had done work for her in the past. "He'll be madly busy right now, with all the tourist trade, so it could take him a few months. But if Yee Tai-tai telephones me when Mr. Yee has a free moment, I'll take him. He'll get them done faster if he knows it's for a friend of mine." As she was going, she left her phone number on the table. While his wife was at the door, seeing Chia-chih out, Mr. Yee would surely have time to copy it down for himself. Then, over the next couple of days, he could find an opportunity to call her—during office hours, when Mr. Mai would be out at work. And they could take it from there.

That evening a light drizzle had been falling. Huang Lei drove her back home and they went back into the house together, where everybody was nervously waiting for news of the evening's triumph. Resplendent in the high-society costume in which she had performed so supremely, she wanted everyone to stay on to celebrate with her, to carouse with her until morning. None of the male students were dancers, but a bowl of soup at one of those small, all-night restaurants and a long walk through the damp night would do just as well. Anything to avoid bed.

Instead, a quiet gradually fell over the assembled company. There was whispering in a couple of corners, and secretive, tittering laughter; laughter she had heard before. They had been talking it over behind her back for some time, she realized.

"Apparently, Liang Jun-sheng is the only one who has any experience," Lai Hsiu-chin, the only other girl in the group, told her.

Liang Jun-sheng.

Of course. He was the only one who had been inside a brothel.

But given that she had already determined to make a sacrifice of herself, she couldn't very well resent him for being the only candidate for the job.

And that evening, while she basked in the heady afterglow of her success, even Liang Jun-sheng didn't seem quite as repellent as usual. One by one, the others saw the way the thing would go; one by one they slipped away, until the two of them were left alone. And so the show went on.

Days passed. Mr. Yee did not call. In the end, she decided to telephone Yee Tai-tai, who sounded listless, offhand: she'd been too busy to go shopping in the last few days, but she'd give her another ring in a day or two.

Did Yee Tai-tai suspect something? Had she discovered her husband in possession of Chia-chih's phone number? Or had they had bad news from the Japanese? After two weeks tormented by worry, she finally received a jubilant phone call from Yee Tai-tai: to say goodbye. She was sorry they were in such a hurry that there'd be no time to meet before they left, but they would love to have her and her husband visit in Shanghai. They must come for a good long time, so they could all go on a trip to Nanking together. Wang Ching-wei's plan to go back to Nanking to form a government must have temporarily run aground,

Chia-chih speculated, and forced them to lie low for a while.

Huang Lei was by now in serious trouble, up to his eyes in debt. And when his family cut off his allowance on hearing that he was cohabiting with a dancing girl in Hong Kong, the scheme's finances collapsed.

The thing with Liang Jun-sheng had been awkward from the start; and now that she was so obviously regretting the whole business, the rest of the group began to avoid her. No one would look her in the eye.

"I was an idiot," she said to herself, "such an idiot."

Had she been set up, she wondered, from the very beginning of this dead-end drama?

From this point on, she kept her distance not only from Liang Jun-sheng, but also from their entire little group. All the time she was with them, she felt they were eyeing her curiously—as if she were some kind of freak, or grotesque. After Pearl Harbor, the sea lanes reopened and all her classmates transferred to Shanghai. Although it, too, had been occupied by the Japanese, its colleges were still open; there was still an education (of sorts) to be had. She did not go with them, and did not try to find them when she got there herself.

For a long time, she agonized over whether she had caught something from Liang Jun-sheng.

Not long after reaching Shanghai, however, the students made contact with an underground worker called Wu—doubtless an alias—who, as soon as he heard about the high-ranking connection they had made, naturally encouraged them to pursue their scheme. And when they approached her, she resolved to do her duty and see the thing through.

In truth, every time she was with Yee she felt cleansed, as if by a scalding hot bath; for now everything she did was for the cause.

They must have posted someone to watch the entrance to the café, and alert everyone the instant his car drew up. When she'd arrived, she hadn't spotted anyone loitering about. The P'ing-an Theater directly opposite would have been an obvious choice, its corridor of pillars offering the perfect cover for a lookout. People were, in any case, always hanging around theater entrances; one could easily wait there without arousing suspicion. But it was a little too far away to identify clearly the occupant of a car parked on the other side of the road.

A delivery bike, apparently broken down, was parked by the entrance to a leather goods shop next door. Its owner—a man of around thirty, with a crew cut—was bent over the mechanism, trying to repair it. Though she couldn't see his face clearly, she was fairly sure he wasn't someone she had seen before. She somehow doubted the bike was the getaway vehicle. There were some things they didn't tell her, and some she didn't ask. But she had heard that members of her old group had been chosen for the job. Even with Wu's help and connections, though, they might not have been able to get hold of a car for afterward. If that car with a charcoal tank stayed where it was, parked just up from the café, it might turn out to be theirs. In which case it would be Huang Lei at the wheel. As she'd approached the café from behind the vehicle, she hadn't seen the driver.

She suspected that Wu didn't have much faith in them: he was probably afraid they were too inexperienced, that they'd get caught and fall to pieces in an interrogation, implicating other people in the process. Chia-chih was sure he was more than a one-man operation here in Shanghai, but he'd been K'uang Yu-min's only point of contact throughout.

He'd promised to let them join his network. Maybe this was their test.

"Before they fire, they get so close the gun's almost up against the body," K'uang Yu-min had once told her, smiling. "They don't shoot from a distance, like in the movies."

This had probably been an attempt to reassure her that they wouldn't cut everyone around him down in an indiscriminate hail of fire. Even if she survived a bullet wound, it would cripple her for life. She'd rather die.

The moment had almost arrived, bringing with it a sharp taste of anticipation.

Her stage fright always evaporated once the curtain was up.

But this waiting was a torment. Men, at least, could smoke through their tension. Opening her handbag, she took out a small bottle of perfume and touched the stopper behind her ears. Its cool, glassy edge felt like her only point of contact with tangible reality. An instant later she caught the scent of Cape Jasmine.

She took off her coat and dabbed some more perfume in the crooks of her elbows. Before she'd had time to put it back on, she saw, through the tiers of a white display-model wedding cake in the window, a car parked outside the café. It was his.

She gathered up her coat and handbag, and walked out with them over her arm. By the time she approached, the driver had opened the door for her. Mr. Yee was sitting in the middle of the backseat.

"I'm late, I know," he muttered, stooping slightly in apology.

She sent him a long, accusing look, then got in. After the driver had returned to his seat, Mr. Yee told him to drive to Ferguson Road—presumably to the apartment where their last assignation had taken place.

"I need to get to a jeweler's first," she told him in a low voice. "I want to replace a diamond stud that's fallen out of one of my earrings. There's a place just here. I would have gone before you got here, but I was afraid I might miss you. So I ended up waiting for ages on my own, like an idiot."

He laughed. "I'm sorry—just as I was leaving, a couple of people I needed to see showed up." He leaned forward to speak to the chauffeur: "Go back to where we just came from." They had already driven some distance away.

"Everything's always so difficult," she pouted. "We're never private at home, there's never a chance to say a word to each other. I want to go back to Hong Kong. Can you get me a boat ticket?"

"Missing the husband?"

"Don't talk to me about him!"

She had told Mr. Yee she was taking revenge for her husband's indiscretion with a dancing girl.

As they sat next to each other in the back of the car, he folded his arms so that his elbow nudged against the fullest part of her breast. This was a familiar trick of his: to sit primly upright while covertly enjoying the pleasurable softness of her.

She twisted around to look out the window, to tell the chauffeur exactly where to stop. The car made a U-turn at the next crossroads, and then another a little farther on to get them back to the P'ing-an, the only respectable second-run cinema in the city. The building's dull red facade curved inward, like a sickle blade set upon the street corner. Opposite was Commander K'ai's Café again, with the Siberian Leather Goods Store and the Green House Ladies' Clothing Emporium next, each fronted by two large display windows filled with glamorously dressed mannequins bent into all manner of poses beneath neon signs. The next-door establishment was smaller and far more nondescript. Although the sign over the door said JEWELER'S, its single display window was practically empty.

He told the chauffeur to stop the car, then got out and followed her inside. Though, in her high-heeled shoes, she was half a head taller than him, he clearly did not mind the disparity in their heights. Tall men, she had found in her experience, liked girls who were small, while short men seemed to prefer their women to tower over them—perhaps out of a desire for balance. She knew he was watching her, and so slightly exaggerated the swivel of her hips as she sashayed through the glass doors like a sea dragon.

An Indian dressed in a Western-style suit greeted them. Though the shop was small, its interior was light, high-ceilinged, and almost entirely bare. It was fitted out with just one waist-high glass showcase, toward the back, in which were displayed some birthstones, one for each month of the year—semiprecious yellow quartz, or red or blue gems made of sapphire or ruby dust, supposed to bring good luck.

She took out of her bag a pear-shaped ruby earring, at the top of which a diamond-studded leaf was missing one stone.

"We can get one to match it," the Indian said, after taking a look.

When she asked how much it would cost and when it would be ready, Mr. Yee added: "Ask him if he has any decent rings." As he had chosen to study in Japan, rather than Britain or the United States, he felt uncomfortable speaking English and always got other people to interpret for him.

She hesitated. "Why?"

He smiled. "I said I wanted to buy you a ring, didn't I? A diamond ring—a decent one."

After another pause, she gave an almost stoic, resigned smile, then softly asked: "Do you have any diamond rings?"

The Indian shouted a startling, incomprehensible stream of what sounded like Hindi upstairs, then escorted them up.

To one side of the cream-colored back wall of the showroom was a door leading to a pitch-dark staircase. The office was on a little mezzanine set between the two floors of the building, with a shallow balcony overlooking the shop floor—presumably for surveillance purposes. The wall immediately to their left as they entered was hung with two mirrors of different sizes, each painted with multicolored birds and flowers and inscribed with gilded Chinese calligraphy: THIS ROC WILL SURELY SOAR TEN THOUSAND MILES. CONGRATULATIONS, MR. BADA, ON YOUR GRAND OPENING. RESPECTFULLY, CH'EN MAO-K'UN. Too tall for the room's sloping ceiling, a third large mirror, decorated with a phoenix and peonies, had been propped up against another wall.

To the front of the room, a desk had been placed along the ebony railing, with a telephone and a reading lamp resting on top. Next to it was a tea table on which sat a typewriter, covered with an old piece of glazed cloth. A second, squat Indian, with a broad ashen-brown face and a nose squashed like a lion's muzzle, stood up from his round-backed armchair to move chairs over for them.

"So it is diamond rings you are interested in. Sit down, please, sit down." He waddled slowly off to a corner of the room, his stomach visibly preceding him, then bent over a low green, ancient-looking safe.

This, clearly, was not a high-class establishment. Though Mr. Yee appeared unfazed by his dingy surroundings, Chia-chih felt a twinge of embarrassment that she had brought him here. These days, she'd heard, some shops were just a front for black marketers or speculators.

Wu had selected this store for its proximity to Commander K'ai's Café. As she'd walked up the stairs, it had occurred to her that on his way back down they would catch him as easily as a turtle in a jar. As he would probably insist on walking in front of her, he would step first into the showroom. There, a couple of male customers browsing the display cabinet would suddenly move out to block his way. But two men couldn't spend too long pretending to choose cheap cuff links, tie pins, and trinkets for absent lady-friends; they couldn't dawdle indecisively like girls. Their entrance needed to be perfectly timed: neither too late nor too early. And once they were in, they had to stay in. Patrolling up and down outside was not an option; his chauffeur would quickly get suspicious. Their best delaying tactic was probably gazing at the window display of the leather shop next door, several yards behind the car.

Sitting to one side of the desk, she couldn't help turning to look down over the balcony. Only the shop window fell within her line of vision. As the window was clear and its glass shelves empty, she could see straight out to the pavement, and to the edge of the car parked next to it.

Then again, perhaps two men shopping alone would look far too conspicuous. They might draw the attention not only of the chauffeur, but also of Mr. Yee himself, from the balcony upstairs, who might then grow suspicious and delay his return downstairs. A stalemate would be catastrophic. Perhaps they would catch him instead at the entrance to the shop. In which case their timing would need to be even more perfect. They would need to approach at a walk, as the sound of running footsteps would instantly alert the chauffeur. Mr. Yee had brought only his driver with him, so perhaps the latter was doubling as a bodyguard.

Or maybe the two of them would split up, one of them lingering in front of the Green House Ladies' Clothing Emporium arm in arm with Lai Hsiu-chin, her eyes glued to the window display. A girl could stand for minutes on end staring at clothes she couldn't afford, while her boyfriend waited impatiently, his back to the shop window, looking around him.

All these scenarios danced vaguely through her mind, even as she realized that none of this was her concern. She could not lose the feeling that, upstairs in this little shop, she was sitting on top of a powder keg that was about to blow her sky-high. A slight tremble was beginning to take hold of her legs.

The shop assistant had gone back downstairs. The boss was much darker skinned than his assistant; they did not look to be father and son. The younger man had saggy, stubbled, pouchlike cheeks and heavy-lidded, sleepy-looking eyes. Though not tall, he was built sturdily enough to serve, if necessity arose, as security guard. The position of the jewelry cabinet so near the back of the shop and the bare window display suggested that they were afraid of being robbed, even in daylight; a padlock hung by the door, for use at night. So there must be something of value on the premises: probably gold bars, U.S. dollars, and silver.

She watched as the Indian brought out a black velvet tray, around a foot long, inlaid with rows of diamond rings. She and Mr. Yee leaned in.

Seeing their lack of interest—neither picked one up to have a closer look—the proprietor put the tray back in the safe. "I've this one, too," he added, opening a small blue velvet box. Set deep within was a pink diamond, the size of a pea.

No one was selling pink diamonds at the moment, she remembered Yee Tai-tai saying. After her initial astonishment had passed, she felt a rush of relief—that the shop had, in the end, come through for her. Until the pink diamond, she had looked like an incompetent bounty hunter, a Cantonese nobody dragging her powerful Shanghai sugar daddy to a tatty gemstone boutique. Of course, the moment the gun sounded, everything—including all peripheral thoughts of plausibility, of pride—would shatter. Although she understood this well enough, she could not allow herself to think about it, for fear that he would see the terror on her face.

She picked up the ring. He laughed softly as he looked at the stone in her hand: "Now that's more like it." She felt a numb chill creeping up the back of her head; the display windows downstairs and the glass door between them seemed to be broadening out, growing taller, as if behind her were an enormous, two-story-high expanse of brilliant, fragile glass, ready to disintegrate at any moment. But even as she felt almost dizzy with the precariousness of her situation, the shop seemed to be blanketing her in torpor. Inside she could hear only the muffled buzz of the city outside—because of the war, there were far fewer cars on the road than usual; the sounding of a horn was a rarity. The warm, sweet air inside the office pressed soporifically down on her like a quilt. Though she was vaguely aware that something was about to happen, her heavy head was telling her that it must all be a dream.

She examined the ring under the lamplight, turning it over in her fingers. Sitting by the balcony, she began to imagine that the bright windows and door visible behind her were a cinema screen across which an action movie was being shown. She had always hated violent films; as a child, she had turned her back whenever a scene became grisly.

"Six carats. Try it on," the Indian urged.

She decided to enjoy the drowsy intimacy of this jeweler's den. Her eyes flitted to the reflection of her foot, nestling amid clumps of peonies, in the mirror propped against the wall, then back to the fabulous treasure—worthy, surely, of a tale from the *Thousand and One Nights*—on her finger. She turned the ring this way, then that, comparing it to the rose red of her nail varnish. Though it seemed pale and small next to her brightly lacquered nails, inside the gloomy office it had an alluring sparkle, like a star burning pink in dusk light. She registered a twinge of regret that it was to be no more than a prop in the short, penultimate scene of the drama unfolding around it.

"So what do you think?" Mr. Yee said.

"What do you think?"

"I'm no expert. I'm happy if you like it."

"Six carats. I don't know whether there are any faults in it. I can't see any."

They leaned in together over the ring, talking and laughing like an engaged couple. Although she had been educated in Canton, the earliest treaty port to open to British traders, the schools there had not attached as much importance to teaching English as they did in Hong Kong, and she always spoke the language in timid, low tones. Sensing her lack of linguistic confidence, the proprietor decided to spare her his usual negotiating preamble on the whys-and-wherefores of diamond-costing. A price was quickly agreed upon: eleven gold bars, to be delivered tomorrow. If any individual bars turned out to fall below the regulation weight, Mr. Yee pledged to make up the difference; likewise, the jeweler promised to reimburse them for any that were too heavy. The entire transaction—trading gold for diamonds—felt like another detail stolen from the *Arabian Nights*.

She worried that the whole thing had been wrapped up too quickly. They probably weren't expecting her and Yee to reemerge so soon. Dialogue, she knew, was the best filler of stage time.

"Shall we ask for a receipt?" He would probably be thinking of sending someone over tomorrow, to deliver the gold and pick up the ring.

The Indian was already writing one out. The ring had also been taken off and returned to him.

They sat back next to each other in their chairs, relaxing in the postnegotiation détente.

She laughed softly. "These days no one wants anything but gold. They don't even want a cash deposit."

"Just as well. I never carry any on me."

She knew, from her experience of living with the Yees, that it was always the aides who covered incidental costs—it was a minister's privilege never to dig into his own pockets. Today, of course, he had come out alone, and therefore penniless, because of the need for secrecy.

The English say that power is an aphrodisiac. She didn't know whether this was true; she herself was entirely oblivious to its attractions. They also say that the way to a man's heart is through his stomach; that a man will fall easy prey to a woman who can cook. Somewhere in the first decade or two of the twentieth century, a well-known Chinese scholar was supposed to have added that the way to a woman's heart is through her vagina. Though his name escaped her, she could remember the analogy he had devised in defense of male polygamy: "A teapot is always surrounded by more than one cup."

•

She refused to believe that an intellectual would come out with something so vulgar. Nor did she believe the saying was true, except perhaps for desperate old prostitutes or merry widows. In her case, she had found Liang Jun-sheng repellent enough before the whole thing began, and afterward even more so.

Though maybe that was not a valid example, because Liang Jun-sheng had been anxious, insecure, painfully aware of her dislike from the outset. His obvious sense of inferiority only grew as things went along between them, increasing her contempt for him.

Surely she hadn't fallen in love with Yee? Despite her fierce skepticism toward the idea, she found herself unable to refute the notion entirely; since she had never been in love, she had no idea what it might feel like. Because, since her midteens, she had been fully occupied in repelling romantic offensives, she had built up a powerful resistance to forming emotional attachments. For a time, she had thought she might be falling for K'uang Yu-min, but she ended up hating him—for turning out just like the others.

The two occasions she had been with Yee, she

had been so tense, so taken up in saying her lines that there had been no opportunity to ask herself how she actually felt. At the house, she had to be constantly on her guard. Every night she was expected to stay up socializing as late as everyone else. When she was finally released back to the privacy of her own room, she would gulp down a sleeping pill to guarantee herself a good night's sleep. Though K'uang Yu-min had given her a small bottle of them, he had told her to avoid taking them if she possibly could, in case anything were to happen in the morning for which a clear head would be required. But without them, she was tormented by insomnia, something she had never suffered from in the past.

Only now, as this last, tense moment of calm stretched infinitely out, on this cramped balcony, the artificial brightness of its lamplight contrasting grubbily with the pale sky visible through the door and windows downstairs, could she permit herself to relax and inquire into her own feelings. Somehow, the nearby presence of the Indian, bent over his writing desk, only intensified her sense of being entirely alone with her lover. But now was not the moment to ask herself whether she loved him; instead, she needed to—

He was gazing off into the middle distance, a faintly sorrowful smile on his face. He had never dared dream such happiness would come his way in middle age. It was, of course, his power and position that he had principally to thank; they were an inseparable part of him. Presents, too, were essential, though they needed to be distributed at the correct moments. Given too soon, they carried within an insulting insinuation of greed. Though he knew perfectly well the rules of the game they were playing, he had to permit himself a brief moment of euphoria at the prize that had fallen into his lap; otherwise, the entire exercise was meaningless.

He was an old hand at this: taking his paramours shopping, ministering to their whims, retreating into the background while they made their choices. But there was, she noted again, no cynicism in his smile just then; only sadness. He sat in silhouette against the lamp, seemingly sunk into an attitude of tenderly affectionate contemplation, his downcast eyelashes tinged the dull cream of moths' wings as they rested on his gaunt cheeks.

He really loves me, she thought. Inside, she felt a raw tremor of shock—then a vague sense of loss.

It was too late.

The Indian passed the receipt to him. He placed it inside his jacket.

"Run," she said softly.

For a moment he stared, and then understood everything. Springing up, he barged the door open, steadied himself on the frame, then swung down to grab firm hold of the banister and stumbled down the dark, narrow stairs. She heard his footsteps break into a run, taking the stairs two or three at a time, thudding irregularly over the treads.

Too late. She had realized too late.

The jeweler was obviously bewildered. Conscious of how suspicious their behavior must look, she forced herself to sit still, resisting the temptation to look down.

They listened to the sound of shoes pounding on floor tiles until he burst into their line of vision, shooting out of the glass door like a cannonball. A moment later, the burly shop assistant also emerged into view, following close behind. She was terrified he might attempt to pull Yee back and ask him to explain himself; a delay of even a few seconds would be fatal. Intimidated, perhaps, by the sight of the official car, however, the Indian stopped in the store entrance, staring out, his heavy, muscular silhouette blocking the doorway. After that, all they heard was the screech of an engine, as if the vehicle were rearing up on its back wheels, followed by a bang. The slam of a door, perhaps—or a gunshot? Then the car roared off.

If it had been gunfire, they would have heard more than one shot.

She steadied herself. Quiet returned.

She heaved a sigh of relief; her entire body felt weak, exhausted, as if just recovered from serious illness. Carefully gathering up her coat and handbag, she smiled and nodded as she got up from her chair: "Tomorrow, then." She lowered her voice again, to its normal English-speaking mumble. "He'd forgotten about another appointment, so he needed to hurry."

The jeweler had already taken his eyeglass back out and adjusted the focus to ascertain that the gentleman just left had not first swapped the pink diamond ring for another. He then saw her smilingly out.

She couldn't blame him for wanting to make sure. The negotiations over price had been suspiciously brief and easy.

She hurried down the stairs. When the shop assistant saw her reappear he hesitated, then seemed to decide to say nothing. As she left, however, she heard shouting between upstairs and down.

There were no free pedicabs outside the shop, so she walked on toward Seymour Road. The group surely must have scattered the moment they saw him dash for the car and drive off; they would have realized that the game was up. She couldn't relax; what if someone had been assigned to watch the back door? What if they hadn't seen what had happened at the front, and hadn't yet left the scene? What would happen if she ran into him? But even if he suspected her of treachery, he wouldn't confront her there and then, much less summarily execute her.

She felt surprised that it was still light outside, as if inside the store she had lost all sense of time. The pavement around her was heaving with humanity; pedicab after pedicab rushed past on the road, all of them taken. Pedestrians and vehicles flowed on by, as if separated from her by a wall of glass, and no more accessible than the elegant mannequins in the window of the Green House Ladies' Clothing Emporium—you could look, but you couldn't touch. They glided along, imperviously serene, as she stood on the outside, alone in her agitation.

She was on the watch for a charcoal-fired vehicle drawing suddenly up beside her, and for a hand darting out to pull her inside.

The pavement in front of the P'ing-an Theater was deserted: the audience was not yet spilling out at the end of a show, so no pedicabs were lined up outside, waiting for customers. Just as she was hesitating over which direction to walk in, she turned and saw that some distance away, along the opposite side of the street, an empty pedicab was slowly approaching, a red, blue, and white windmill tied to its handlebar. Seeing her wave and shout at him, the tall young cyclist hurried to cross over, the little windmill spinning faster as he accelerated toward her.

"Yü Garden Road," she told him as she got in.

Fortunately, while she'd been in Shanghai she'd had very little direct contact with the group, and so had never got around to mentioning that she had a relative living on Yü Garden Road. She thought she would stay there a few days, while she assessed the situation.

As the pedicab approached Ching-an Temple, she heard a whistle blow.

"The road's blocked," her cyclist told her.

A middle-aged man in a short mandarin jacket was pulling a length of rope across the street, holding the whistle in his mouth. On the other side of the road, a second, similarly dressed man pulled the other end of the rope straight to seal off the traffic and pedestrians within. Someone was lethargically ringing a bell, the thin, tinny sound barely carrying over the wide street.

Her pedicab driver cycled indomitably up to the rope, then braked and impatiently spun his windmill, before turning around to smile at her.

Three black capes were now sitting around the mahjong table. The nose of the new arrival—Liao Tai-tai—was speckled with white pockmarks.

"Mr. Yee's back," Ma Tai-tai smirked.

"What a wicked liar that Wang Chia-chih is!" Yee Tai-tai complained. "Promising to take us all out to dinner then running away. I'll collapse with hunger if she makes us wait much longer!"

"Mr. Yee." Liao Tai-tai smiled. "Your wife's bankrupted us all today. She'll be the one buying dinner tomorrow."

"Mr. Yee," Ma Tai-tai said, "where's the dinner you promised us last time you won? It's impossible to get a meal out of you."

"Mr. Yee ought to buy us dinner tonight, since we can never get him to accept our invitations," the other black cape said.

He merely smiled. After the maid brought him tea, he knocked his cigarette ash onto the saucer, glancing across at the thick wool curtains covering the wall opposite and wondering how many assassins they could conceal. He was still shaken by the afternoon's events.

Tomorrow he must remember to have them taken down, though his wife was bound to object to something so expensive being sidelined into a storeroom.

It was all her fault, the result of her careless choice of friends. But even he was impressed by how elaborately, how far in advance—two years—the entire trap had been premeditated. The preparations had, indeed, been so perfectly thorough that only a last-minute change of heart on the part of his femme fatale had saved him. So she really had loved him—his first true love. What a stroke of luck.

He could have kept her on. He had heard or read somewhere that all spies are brothers; that spies can feel a loyalty to one another stronger than the causes that divide them. In any case, she was only a student. Of that group of theirs, only one had been in the pay of Chungking, the one who had gotten away—the single glitch in the entire operation. Most likely he'd stepped out of the P'ing-an halfway through a showing, then gone back into the theater once the assassination attempt was aborted. After the area was sealed off, he would have shown the police his ticket stub and then been allowed to slip away. The young man who'd waited with him to do the job had seen him check that the stub was safely stashed along with his cigarettes. It had been agreed in advance that he wouldn't take up room in the getaway car; that afterward he would stroll inconspicuously back into the cinema. After they'd been roughed up a bit, the little idiots came out with the whole story.

Mr. Yee stood behind his wife, watching the

game. After he had stubbed out his cigarette, he took a sip of his tea; still too hot. Though an early night was surely what he needed, he was over-tired, unable to wind down. He was exhausted from sitting by the phone all afternoon waiting for news; he hadn't even had a proper dinner. As soon as he'd reached safety, he'd immediately tele-phoned to get the whole area sealed off. By ten o'clock that evening they'd all been shot. She must have hated him at the end. But real men have to be ruthless. She wouldn't have loved him if he'd been the sentimental type.

And, of course, his hands had been tied—more by Chou Fo-hai than by the Japanese military police. For some time Chou had been directing his own secret-service operation, and saw Gov-ernment Intelligence—Mr. Yee's department—as an irrelevance. Consequently, he kept an oppres-sively close eye on them, always on the lookout for evidence of incompetence. Mr. Yee could imagine all too easily what use Chou would have made of the discovery that the head of Domestic Intelligence had given house-room to an assas-sin's plant.

Now, at least, Chou could find no grounds on

which to reproach him. If he accused him of executing potentially useful witnesses, he could confidently counter that they'd been only students; they weren't experienced spies from whom a slow, reasoned torture could have spilled useful information. And if the executions had been delayed, word of the affair might have gotten out. They would have become patriotic heroes plotting to assassinate a national traitor; a rallying point for popular discontent.

He was not optimistic about the way the war was going, and he had no idea how it would turn out for him. But now that he had enjoyed the love of a beautiful woman, he could die happy—without regret. He could feel her shadow forever near him, comforting him. Even though she had hated him at the end, she had at least felt something. And now he possessed her utterly, primitively—as a hunter does his quarry, a tiger his kill. Alive, her body belonged to him; dead, she was his ghost.

"Take us out to dinner, Mr. Yee! Take us out!" the three black capes chirruped ferociously. "He promised last time!"

"So did Ma Tai-tai," Yee Tai-tai smilingly intervened, "then when we didn't see her for a few days, we forgot all about it."

"Ever the loyal wife." Ma Tai-tai smiled back.

"Look, is Mr. Yee going to take us to dinner or not?"

"Mr. Yee has certainly had a run of luck lately," Ma Tai-tai pronounced, looking at him and smiling again. They understood each other perfectly. She could hardly have failed to notice the two of them disappearing, one after the other. And the girl still wasn't back. He had looked distracted when he returned, the elation still glimmering over his face. This afternoon, she guessed, had been their first assignation.

He reminded himself to drill his wife on the official story he had made up: that Mai Tai-tai had needed to hurry back to Hong Kong to take care of urgent family business. Then, to frighten her a bit with some secret-service patter: that not long after she invited this viper into the bosom of their home, he had received intelligence that she was part of a Chungking spy ring. Just as his people had begun to make further inquiries, he had heard that the Japanese had gotten wind of it. If he hadn't struck first, he would have gotten none of the credit for the intelligence work already done, and the Japanese might have discovered the connection with his wife, and tried to incriminate him. Best lay it on thick, so that she didn't listen to Ma Tai-tai's gossip.

"Take us to dinner, Mr. Yee! Stop getting your wife to do your dirty work."

"My wife gives her own dinners. She's promised you tomorrow."

"We know how busy you are, Mr. Yee. You tell us when you're free, and we'll be there; any day after tomorrow."

"No, take us tonight. How about Lai-hsi?"

"The only edible thing there is the cold buffet."

"German food is boring—nothing but cold cuts. How about somewhere Hunanese, just for a change?"

"Or there's Shu-yü—Ma Tai-tai didn't come with us yesterday."

"I'd rather Chiu-ju—I haven't been there for ages."

"Didn't Yang Tai-tai hold a dinner at Chiu-ju?"

"Last time we went, we didn't have Liao Tai-tai with us. We needed someone from Hunan—we didn't know what to order."

"It's too spicy for me!"

"Then tell the chef to make it less spicy."

"Only cold fish won't eat hot chili!"

Amid the raucous laughter, he quietly slipped out.

AFTERWORD

Ang Lee

To me, no writer has ever used the Chinese language as cruelly as Zhang Ailing (Eileen Chang), and no story of hers is as beautiful or as cruel as "Lust, Caution." She revised the story for years and years—for decades—returning to it as a criminal might return to the scene of a crime, or as a victim might reenact a trauma, reaching for pleasure only by varying and reimagining the pain. Making our film, we didn't really "adapt" Zhang's work, we simply kept returning to her theater of cruelty and love until we had enough to make a movie of it.

Zhang is very specific in the traps her words set. For example, in Chinese we have the figure of the tiger who kills a person. Thereafter, the person's ghost willingly works for the tiger, helping to lure more prey into the jungle. The Chinese phrase for this is *wei hu dzuo chung.* It's a common phrase and was often used to refer to the Chinese who collaborated with the Japanese occupiers during the war. In the story Zhang has Yee allude to this phrase to describe the relationship between men and women. Alive, Chia-chih was his woman; dead, she is his ghost, his *chung.* But perhaps she already was one when they first met, and now, from beyond her grave, she is luring him closer to the tiger. . . .

Interestingly, the word for *tiger's ghost* sounds exactly like the word for *prostitute.* So in the movie, in the Japanese tavern scene, Yee refers to himself with this word. It could refer to his relationship to the Japanese—he is both their whore and their *chung.* But it also means he knows he is already a dead man.

We, the readers of Zhang Ailing, are we her *chung*? Often the transition from one life into the next is made unexpectedly, as an experience of the imagination. Zhang describes the feeling Chia-chih had after performing on stage as a young woman, the rush she felt afterward, that she could barely calm down even after a late-night meal with her friends from the theater and a ride on the upper deck of a tram. When I read that, my mind raced back to my own first experience on the stage, back in 1973 at the Academy of Art in Taipei: the same rush of energy at the end of the play, the same late-night camaraderie, the same wandering. I realized how that experience was central to Zhang's work, and how it could be transformed into film. She understood playacting and mimicry as something by nature cruel and brutal: animals, like her characters, use camouflage to evade their enemies and lure their prey. But mimicry and performance are also ways we open ourselves as human beings to greater experience, indefinable connections to others, higher meanings, art, and the truth.

WHY DID SHE DO IT?

James Schamus

Why did she do it?

The question is itself an admission of the impossibility of ever really answering it.

And yet we ask.

Another, more specific, way of asking:

What act, exactly, does Wang Chia-chih perform at that fateful moment in the jeweler's shop when she decides whether or not to go through with the murder of her lover?

And here, two words—*act* and *perform*—indicate the troubling question Zhang Ailing (Eileen Chang) asks us: for at the crucial moment when we *choose*, when we *decide*, when we *exercise our free will*, are we not also *performing*?

One could say that "Lust, Caution" depicts a heroine who "becomes herself" only when she takes on the identity of another, for only behind the mask of the character Mai Tai-tai can Chia-chih truly desire, and thus truly live—playacting allows her to discover her one real love. But this is too reductive. For the performer always, by definition, performs *for* someone. And that audience, no matter how entranced, is always complicit: it knows deep down that the performance isn't real, but it also knows the cathartic truth the performer strives for is attainable only when that truth is, indeed, *performed*. Yee doesn't simply desire Mai Tai-tai while suspecting she is not who she says she is; it is precisely *because* he suspects her that he desires her. In this sense his desire is the same as hers: he wants to *know* her. And so lust and caution are, in Zhang's work, functions of each other, not because we desire what is dangerous, but because our love is, no matter how earnest, an *act*, and therefore always an object of suspicion.

If Chia-chih's act at the end of the story is indeed an expression of love, it paradoxically destroys the very theatrical contract that made the performance of that love possible—in killing off her fictional character, she effectively kills herself. Her act is thus a negation of the very idea that it could be acknowledged, understood, explained, or reciprocated by its audience.[1]

I think one of the things that drew Ang Lee, and the rest of us with him, toward Zhang Ailing's work was a feeling that her writing itself is just this kind of "act"—a profound cry of protest against the warring structures of domination that so cataclysmically shaped midcentury China and made her life a long series of displacements. "Lust, Caution" is of course not a work of autobiography, but in it we see the shape of Zhang's life, and its terrible disorientations, ghosted behind almost every line.

---

[1] I get much of this sense of the "act" from the philosopher Slavoj Žižek. See his *Enjoy Your Symptom!: Jacques Lacan in Hollywood and Out* (New York: Routledge, 2001): "The act differs from an active intervention (action) in that it radically transforms its bearer (agent): the act is not simply something that I 'accomplish'—after an act, I'm literally 'not the same as before' . . . in it, the subject is annihilated and subsequently reborn (or not) . . ." (p. 44). For Žižek, the act is a supreme form of feminine rejection: "we shouldn't forget that the paradigmatic case of such an act is feminine: Antigone's 'No!' to Creon, to state power; her act is literally suicidal, she excludes herself from the community, whereby she offers nothing new, no positive program—she just insists on her unconditional demand" (p. 46). I discuss this idea further in *Gertrud: The Moving Word* (Seattle: University of Washington Press, forthcoming 2008).

* * *

Like her heroine, Wang Chia-chih, Zhang was a student in Hong Kong during the Pacific War's early years; the Japanese invasion of Hong Kong in 1941 cut short her English studies at the University of Hong Kong, precipitating her return to her aunt and mother's home in Shanghai—a home to which she had fled a few years earlier after a stay with her opium-addicted, abusive father. In Shanghai she married her first husband, a philanderer who served in the collaborationist government; when the Japanese were defeated, he fled and took up with another woman. Like Chia-chih, Zhang had earlier tried to get to London, but the war eclipsed those plans, too. In 1952, she moved to Hong Kong, and from there to the United States, where she died, in 1995, at the age of seventy-five, in Los Angeles. A precocious and accomplished literary genius, she wrote masterpieces in her early twenties. She continued to write, both in Chinese and English, into the 1970s, and though her works were banned for a long time in Mainland China, she has remained a revered and widely read author throughout the Chinese-speaking world.

Zhang did not just transmute her private sagas into art; she took the dominant cultural and po lit-ical myths of her day and followed her char acters to their bitterest ends as they fulfilled those myths. In this, she made use in particular of another "Shanghai Xiaoxie" (Shanghai Miss) of the 1920s and '30s, a woman who was per haps the greatest star the Chinese cinema has ever produced: Ruan Lingyu. Ruan, even in her day, was something of a mythic figure, revered with an uncommon fer-vor—it is said, for ex ample, that at her funeral in 1935 the proces sion was more than two miles long. Facing a public scandal caused by a ne'er-do-well for mer lover, she killed herself at the age of twenty-five. Her death was a national trauma, made all the more disturbing by the fact that in her last film, the wildly popular *New Woman* (1935, directed by Cai Chu-sheng), she portrayed a character who also met her death at her own hand—a character based on a real actress, Ai Xia, who had herself committed suicide.[2] Wang

[2] See Zhang Zhen, *An Amorous History of the Silver Screen: Shanghai Cinema 1896–1937* (Chicago: University of Chicago Press, 2005), p. 266. The Hong Kong filmmaker Stanley Kwan has made a remarkable film about Ruan Lingyu, titled *Center Stage* (1992).

Chia-chih, like Ruan Lingyu, is a woman caught up in a game of cinematic and literary mirrors, a game that has now ensnared Ang Lee as he reflects his own cinematic mirror onto Zhang Ailing's remarkable work.

ALSO AVAILABLE

LUST, CAUTION:

The Story, the Screenplay, and the Making of the Film

THE DELUXE EDITION INCLUDES:

A preface by Ang Lee • An introduction by James Schamus on adapting *Lust, Caution* for the screen • Eileen Chang's original story • Wang Hui Ling & James Schamus' screenplay for the film • Production Notes • 8 pages of stills from the film

ISBN-10: 0-375-42524-1 / ISBN-13: 978-0-375-42524-0
$22.95 (Can. $29.95)

AVAILABLE WHEREVER BOOKS ARE SOLD

PANTHEON BOOKS www.pantheonbooks.com